"I was born in London in 1946 and grew up in a sweet shop in Essex. For several years I worked as a graphic designer, but in 1980 I decided to concentrate on writing and illustrating books for children.

My wife, Annette, and I have two grown-up children, Ben and Amanda, and we have put down roots in Suffolk.

I haven't recently counted how many books there are with my name on the cover but Percy the Park Keeper accounts for a good many of them. I'm reliably informed that they have sold more than three million copies. Hooray!

I didn't realise this when I invented Percy, but I can now see that he's very like my mum's dad, my grandpa. I even have a picture of him giving a ride to my brother and me in his old home-made wooden wheelbarrow!"

NICK BUTTERWORTH

# PERCY'S FRIEND
# THE SQUIRRELS

# NICK BUTTERWORTH

HarperCollins *Children's Books*

*Thanks Graham Daldry. You're a wizard.*

*Thanks Atholl McDonald. You're a hero!*

First published in Great Britain by HarperCollins Publishers Ltd in 2001
ISBN-13: 978 0 00 778263 5
ISBN-10: 0 00 778263 2

Text and illustrations copyright © Nick Butterworth 2001
The author asserts the moral right to be identified as the author of the work.

Visit our website at: www.harpercollinschildrensbooks.co.uk

Printed and bound in Thailand by Imago

# MY FRIENDS THE SQUIRRELS

Squirrels are bright and quick thinking. They move quickly too and not just over the ground. They seem to be able to whizz straight up a tree as if it were a fallen log!

They like to explore, which can get them into trouble sometimes. I remember an awful kerfuffle once, when a squirrel got stuck in a rabbit hole. Unlike the mole, squirrels are not good at going backwards. I believe it's something to do with bushy tails.

Squirrels can be very forgetful. They never, never seem to remember where they have stored their food. Which reminds me, I put a sandwich down a moment ago. You haven't seen it, have you?

Once, when I was on my way to pick some apples, I noticed three squirrels up in the branches of an oak tree, collecting acorns. I thought how nice it would be, if I could pick my apples like that.

Suddenly, I had a brainwave. My apples could be picked in exactly the same way!

Now, in the autumn, the squirrels help to pick all those apples that are so hard to get at the tops of the trees. And I pick the easy ones that I can reach without having to use my ladder.

It's a very good arrangement. It is strange though. I've noticed a lot more apples have little teeth marks in them than when I used to pick them by myself.

# SQUIRRELS REALLY LIKE ...

Balancing. They seem to be able to balance on just about anything, although there have been one or two accidents on my washing line!

Nuts. Not just acorns and beech nuts. They like peanuts, coconut and hazelnuts too. And they don't mind if they're covered in chocolate!

# SQUIRRELS DON'T LIKE ...

Lightning. I love to watch it myself,
but I suppose it's different if you live at
the top of a tall tree!

Being underground.
Here are two squirrels with their friend,
the mole. Guess which is which!

Everybody loves tobogganing! Well, nearly everybody. Actually, I don't think the owl likes it all that much. And I don't think my Auntie Joyce is too keen...But I think just about everyone else loves tobogganing.

The squirrels are especially good at it. Some of their high-speed acrobatics are just amazing.

I think the squirrels would agree though, that their steering of a toboggan is not quite so amazing.

In fact, sometimes, it's not at all amazing.

It's amusing.

I've got lots of pictures in my photo album.

This palm tree is made from flower pots and fern leaves. The two little monkeys are made from squirrels!

The little monkeys broke my flower pots!

Here are some I took of my good friends, the squirrels.

Squirrels do stop for a rest sometimes. These four were caught napping in my potting shed.

My old wheelbarrow makes a perfect exercise wheel!

The squirrels have great fun playing a game
they call 'Acorn Surprise'.
Sometimes it can be called
'Pine Cone Surprise' or
'Conker Surprise'. It just
depends what kind of tree
they are sitting in.
It goes like this...

They sit quietly on a branch and wait for somebody to walk underneath. Then they drop an acorn (or a pine cone or a conker) onto the person below.

Actually, I had to ask them not to drop conkers after they dropped some rather big ones that were still in their spiky cases. 'Conker Surprise' became 'Conker Ouch!'

It's not that far from here to . . .
It's just a short leap through the air.
This tree to . . .
I'll be all right.
I'll grab that branch and hold on tight . . .
The distance doesn't bother me.

I could . . .

The gap that makes me

Hang around

Is the one between me . . .

there

that

somersault it . . .

see!

and the ground!

# FAVOURITE PLACES

The squirrels seem to have quite a few favourite places. One that I can think of is a small clearing in the middle of the pine wood which they call the Mushroom Field. They call it that because of the lovely big mushrooms that grow there.

On a misty, autumn morning, if you get up early enough, that's where you'll find the squirrels, having a very tasty breakfast!

Now, if I asked what you would
expect to find waving in the breeze
at the top of a flag pole, the sensible
answer would be a flag. You probably
wouldn't say squirrels! Not unless
you have been to *this* park.

But if you have, you might have
seen some of my squirrel friends
enjoying the view from another of
their favourite places. They tell
me there is just enough room for
three. Four is a bit of a squash.

I say, there doesn't look to be
room even for one! I tell them
to be very careful. I suggest
that they might be just a little
safer leaping through the
branches of the big oak tree
house which, of course, is
where they live.

Here they are, my friends the squirrels.
Are they collecting food here, or are
they just playing a game? Actually, if
I know anthing about squirrels, they're
probably doing both at the same time!